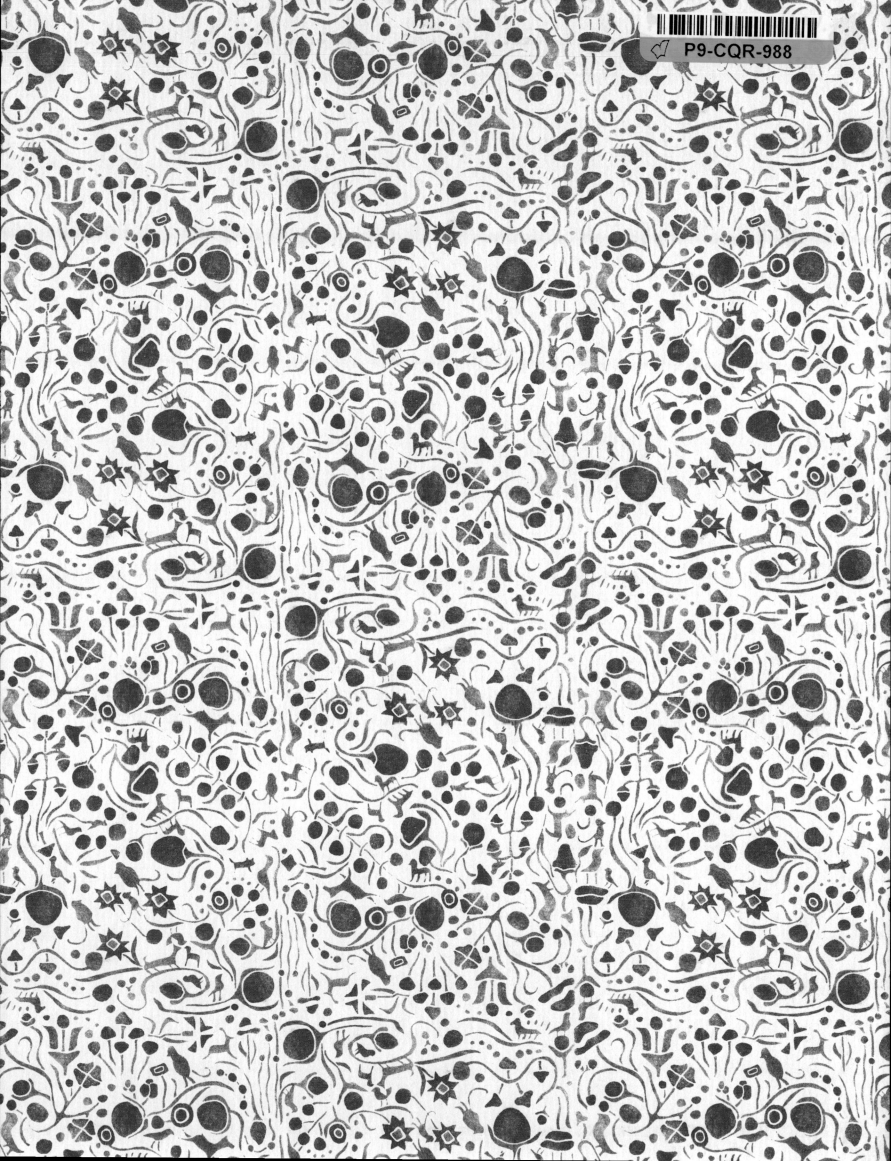

LITTLE NIGHT CAT

For my dog, Dunni, who also liked cats. —S. D.

First published in the United States, Great Britain, Canada, Australia, and New Zealand in 2016
by NorthSouth Books Inc., an imprint of NordSüd Verlag AG, CH-8005 Zürich, Switzerland.
Distributed in the United States by NorthSouth Books Inc., New York 10016.
Library of Congress Cataloging-in-Publication Data is available.
Printed in Latvia by Livonia Print, Riga, May 2016.
ISBN: 978-0-7358-4266-3
1 3 5 7 9 · 10 8 6 4 2
www.northsouth.com

SONJA DANOWSKI

LITTLE NIGHT CAT

North
South

It was a very special Sunday. The grand summer party would be taking place in the animal shelter. There were still a few hours to go, so Tony could stay cozily in bed with his toys if he wanted to; but he had something important to do. He quickly got up and put on his red robe.

He ran downstairs, sat at the kitchen table, and drew a panther.
He did it really well. It was for a raffle at the animal shelter. The cats
and dogs needed food and medicine, and that cost a lot of money.

"A picture of a panther will certainly not be enough," Tony said to
himself. Then he had an idea. "Mom, I'm going to give them my toys.
When people see my stuffed animals, they'll want to buy all the tickets!"

"But you love them so much! I don't think that's a good idea," said
Tony's mother. "Yes it is, because my stuffed animals also want to help,"
insisted Tony.

So they packed all his toys in a big bag.

They reached the animal shelter at noon.

Mom carried the bag into the entrance hall. There were already a few other raffle prizes: books and useful things such as eggcups and candles. But next to Tony's cuddly toys they were just consolation prizes.

Anne, the director of the animal shelter, was absolutely delighted.

"Such wonderful stuffed animals! How can I ever thank you, Tony? And your drawing of a panther is much too beautiful to give away. We'll put it in a place of honor in the cats' room. Come on, let's hang it up."

In the meantime, Mom got her cello from the car, because there was going to be a little concert.

In the cats' room, the cats were enjoying their midday nap—curled up in their favorite sleeping places.

"Hello, cats," whispered Tony. "Don't let us disturb you. We're just bringing you a panther."

A big tomcat with silky gray fur sleepily opened his eyes. He nodded, licked his paw, and then cautiously crept over to Tony.

"This is Valentine. He's a bit shy," Anne explained. Valentine sat down and immediately closed his eyes again. Tony gently stroked his head and quietly hummed a little tune. "Do you like the song?" he asked. "It's called *Little Night Cat*."

Valentine purred contentedly.

Outside, the summer party was beginning.

The sun was shining, and in the courtyard the decorations were fluttering in the breeze. Mom and Anne were on the stage, and they played the specially composed cat song. It sounded beautiful, and when Anne's dog howled an accompaniment, everybody laughed.

After the concert, the visitors crowded around the stand where Tony's toys were being raffled.

By early afternoon, all the tickets had sold, and the little tin collection container was full to the brim with money. Tony spent the whole afternoon outside the window of the cats' room. Valentine looked at him through the glass. When the sun slowly sank, the lucky winners went home with Tony's stuffed animals.

At night, in his bed, Tony thought about Valentine and about his toys. His bed felt empty. Uncomfortably empty. Tony got up and called out, "Mommy, I can't sleep!"

Mom was in the bathroom. He didn't have to say anything else. Mommy knew at once what needed to be done. She held Tony's hand, took him into the living room, and spread a blanket over the sofa.

"You can lie down on the warm cushions—or would you like to help me look?"

"What are we looking for?" asked Tony. Mom climbed onto a chair, and from the top shelf of the cupboard, she passed a suitcase down to Tony.

"See if Paul is in there."

Tony put the case on the table and opened it. In the case was Mommy's beloved stuffed cat, Paul! He was more than thirty years old, and his fur was worn-out in places. Life had left its mark on him. Even the poor cat's two button eyes had fallen out.

Tony stroked Paul's head. "Poor kitty!"

Tony had an idea. He ran into the bathroom and grabbed the round earrings from Mom's jewelry stand. They were shiny orange, with a black circle in the middle. They were made just for Paul! Mommy sewed the new cat's eyes onto Paul's face.

"Now you look beautiful again," said Tony happily. He wrapped Paul up in a brightly colored little blanket and carried him to the sofa.

The two of them snuggled up on the soft cushions.

"Tomorrow I'll show you where I go to school," said Tony. A moment later, his eyes closed. During the night he dreamed about two gray cats.

The next morning, Mom took Tony to school. Paul sat in the bike basket. "Mommy, will you bring Paul when you pick me up? He doesn't want to stay home by himself."

Mom promised not to leave Paul alone.

After school, Tony waited impatiently for Mom.

There she is! But where is Paul?

"You promised you wouldn't leave him on his own!"

"I know," said Mom, "but Paul refused to come out of his hiding place. Don't worry, Tony, he's not alone. Someone is looking after him."

Tony didn't hear her last words. Disappointed, he climbed onto the bike and didn't say a word all the way home.

Tony was in a very bad mood and slammed the front door.

Two sparkling cat's eyes shone up at him. "Valentine! What are you doing here?" cried Tony in surprise. Valentine was sitting on a stool in the hall. Paul was there too. Tony could hardly believe his eyes.

"Is Valentine going to stay with us, Mommy? For good?"

"Yes, Valentine's going to live here, and we will look after Paul very nicely." Tony's face beamed as Valentine happily licked his paws.

Valentine quickly got used to living in his new home.

When Tony came home from school, Valentine couldn't wait for his best friend to greet him and pet him. Valentine particularly enjoyed hearing Mommy play the cello. Then he'd stretch his paws up in the air and purr next to the climbing tree that Tony and his mother made especially for him.

But one evening when the sun sank down behind the roofs of the town, Valentine suddenly ran out of the balcony door, climbed down the tree, and disappeared.

"He's just gone for an evening walk. He'll come back soon," said Mom. Tony sadly lowered his head.

"But suppose he can't find his way home?"

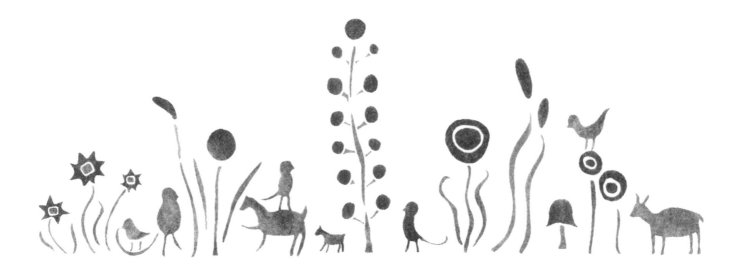

It was very late. Tony was tired, but without Valentine he couldn't get to sleep. He sat outside on the balcony and kept watch for Valentine. Sadly he hummed the cat song to himself.

His eyes were just beginning to close when suddenly he felt something soft against his leg. "Valentine! You heard your song and came home! I'm so happy you're back again! You're my little night cat."

Tony's mind was at rest, and he could go to sleep. Tomorrow there would be a new adventure for him and his two furry friends.

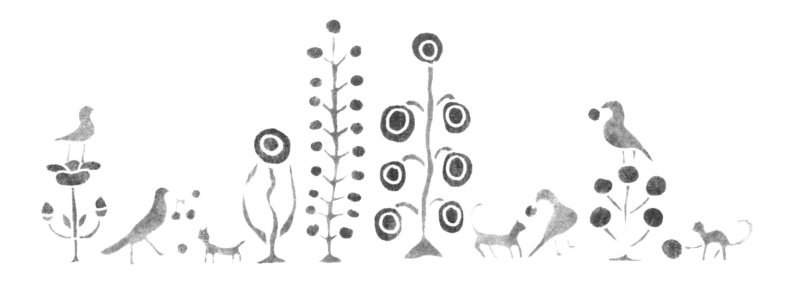

LITTLE NIGHT CAT

Sonja Danowski

SONJA DANOWSKI was born in Iserlohn, Germany. She studied design in Nuremberg and since then has been working in Berlin as an illustrator. Her work focuses especially on picture books, using images to preserve human memories. Her colorful illustrations have won her many international awards, including the Golden Island Award in the Nami Island International Picture Book Illustration Concours 2015. Her first book for NorthSouth Books, *Grandma Lives in a Perfume Village*, was a Batchelder Honor Book.

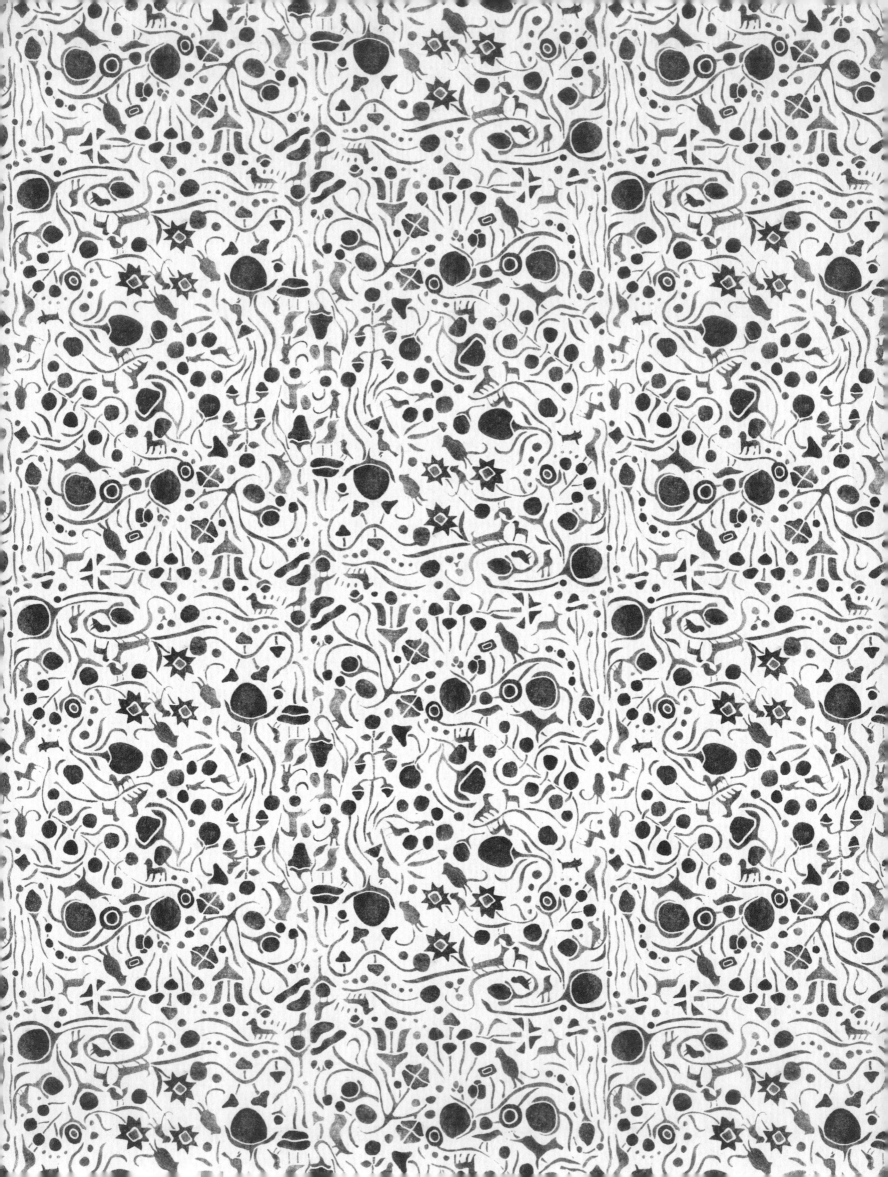